J(

Down on the Farm

By L.S. Winters

Copyright © 2020

L.S. Winters

Cover Illustration by

Mary Tsoukali

ACKNOWLEDGEMENTS

As I continue this journey, I would like to thank everyone who encouraged me along the way. Thank you for believing in me.

CHAPTER ONE

Jo is feeling quite miserable today. She usually likes rainy days. Most rainy days she can sit on the porch and read with her best friend, Alex. If it gets too cold, they move inside. Mom sometimes makes them hot chocolate and they sit and read on the couch.

Today is not one of those days. Jo can't read her book, she has to wear the itchy cardigan Gramma Gladys made her, and Alex hasn't answered any of her text messages. She is trying her best not to cry. Her cat Jimothy has fallen asleep on the couch. Jo should be sitting on the couch reading with Jim and Alex… instead, she is sitting and waiting on the stairs.

The house phone rings. Mom answers it. Jo is excited and hopeful about who it might be.

Finally, maybe Alex is ready to go? Thinks Jo to herself.

Mom smiles and says yes to whoever is on the other end of the line, then puts the phone down. Mom looks up and sees Jo sitting on the stairs, waiting very impatiently.

"C'mon honey, cheer up. I thought you loved going to the farm?" Jo's Mom asks kindly.

"It's rainy, I can't read because we are about to leave, and this cardigan is *so* itchy. Is Alex ready to go?" Jo asks.

"Patience is key, sweetie. Yes, that was her Mom on the phone. She will meet us at the garage."

Jo jumps up and gives her Mom a great big hug and a kiss.

"Bye Jim!"

Jo runs out the front door, red polka dot suitcase in hand and the cardigan flying behind her like a cape.

"Surprise! I win!" shouts Alex when Jo gets to the garage.

Even though Jo was watching the front door, somehow Alex beat her to the car. Alex has a stripy blue suitcase, it's so pretty!

Jo thinks that the drive to the farm is going to take forever. Maybe this is what her mom meant by having patience?

Finally, the rain stops and Jo wonders to herself if this is the same feeling of relief Noah felt when the sun came out again. She rolls down the window when she starts to recognize the fields that are close to Gramma's farm.

Alex copies her on the other side of the car. It smells like freshly cut grass; there are so many more noises near Gramma Gladys' farm! Jo loves it there. Alex leans over and tugs on Jo's cardigan, grabbing her attention.

"What is that funny squawking sound, is someone stepping on a rubber ducky?" asks Alex.

"No, silly! It is the sound of the geese near Gramma Gladys' farm. She calls them Mother Nature's alarm." responds Jo excitedly. "They make noise when people or cars are near the gate. That means we are close!"

The car turns the last corner and crunches its way along a brown sandy road. The trees line up like soldiers on either side of the road. All the way at the end is the big white house. An energetic sheepdog follows them from the gate to the house.

"It's so pretty here! Look at that big porch and the happy sheepdog. No wonder you like it here, Jo!" Alex exclaims with excitement.

The white farmhouse is two stories high with a big wrap-around porch on the ground floor, lots of windows, and a blue pitched roof. Large blue shutters are standing wide open to let all the cool air pass through. There is a beautiful wooden rocking chair by the front door with a two-seater porch swing next to it. The perfect place to read books.

A lady, who Alex thinks must be Jo's Gramma Gladys, walks out of the screen door. She has red hair mixed with grey just like Jo's Mom. She is wearing denim trousers under a big flowy white shirt. Her clothes are covered by a pink apron.

Alex is nervous. Butterflies are flying around in her tummy.

Gramma Gladys has the same smile as Jo, Alex thinks to herself. *I really hope she likes me.*

The car finally pulls up outside the beautiful farmhouse. Jo opens the car door, and the sheepdog eagerly hops in licking her face. Jo and Alex giggle together, calming the butterflies in Alex's tummy.

Alex likes dogs more than cats but hasn't found a way to tell Jo yet.

Gramma Gladys wipes her hands on her apron, calling out, "Jule, stop it now you big ball of fluff. Hello, girls! Welcome to the farm!"

Jo squeals with delight and runs up to her Gramma, giving her a big hug.

"Look at how much you have grown, my
tle bug. One of these days you will be taller than
ne!" Gramma smiles and pinches her cheek.

"Thanks, Gramma. There is someone special
I want you to meet: my best friend in the whole
wide world, Alex!'' Jo turns, motioning Alex to
come closer. "Alex, this is my Gramma Gladys. She
loves adventures just like us!"

Great. Alex feels like she is put on the spot.
Her face is burning hot. The last time she felt this
shy was when she met Jo for the first time. Gramma
Gladys adjusts the red glasses on her nose, smiling
at Alex warmly.

She opens her arms to Alex, welcoming her
in for a hug as well.

"Hello Alex, it's lovely to meet you. Would
you like to come in for a glass of sweet tea and a
sandwich?" Gramma Gladys says as Alex walks
closer. Alex likes how nice Gramma Gladys is.

"Let's get you settled and you can tell me all
about these bikes you two are saving up for.
Beautiful cardigan Jo, but it's way too hot for that
my little bug!" Gramma Gladys gestures them
toward the house. A sigh of relief escapes Jo's lips
as she pulls off the cardigan with glee.

Alex finds Jo's happiness at being here
reassuring. Gramma Gladys sounds kind just like

Jo's Mom, who is very kind. Alex wants pretty red glasses like Gramma Gladys one day.

Alex and Jo grab their bags and run into the farmhouse, saying bye to Jo's Mom and Dad on the way. The smell of freshly baked bread drifts past their noses. Jo's tummy growls loudly. Gramma Gladys hears it and laughs.

"Are you hungry, my dears?" asks Gramma Gladys.

"Yes, Gramma!", chime Jo and Alex.

"Drop off your luggage in the room, then hop right to the kitchen!"

They soon return to the kitchen and see that Gramma has huge sandwiches ready for them, set out with a note saying:

I'll be back in a jiffy!
Bessie the cow is having her calf.
Grampa Mark needed some help with it,
Love G.

As soon as they finish their food, they hear a knock on the kitchen's back door. A little boy walks in. He looks to be the same age as them. He is whistling as he enters the kitchen, and on his head he has a red flat cap that covers the biggest mop of black hair Alex has ever seen. He smiles broadly when he catches sight of the girls, confidently showing no front teeth. He tries to bow like a gentleman. Instead the boy trips, falling on his happy face.

Jo and Alex hop off their chairs laughing, trying their best to help the boy up.

Jo exclaims, "Oh, it's you Jackson!"

The boys' face burns with embarrassment.

"Helloo, Jojo," he says. "Good to thhee ya again!"

Jo smiles back at him happily and says, "I thought you weren't arriving until tomorrow?"

"I couthent wait knowing you'd be on your way," he proudly replies.

Alex thinks he sounds funny. *Did he eat a spoonful of peanut butter to sound like that?*

Jackson looks over to Alex, noticing her for the first time. "Ah, yeth. My mom thaid you would bing a fwend." He extends his hand, "My name ith Jackthon, nithe tah meet yah, Ma'am!"

Alex giggles at how proper he tries to sound. It reminds Alex of when Jo had a British accent, except with a lisp.

"Hi. My name is Alex, I'm Jo's best friend," Alex says as she shakes his hand. "It's nice to meet you, Jackson. Sorry about your face. Can we get you some ice?"

"Naw, but thath mighty kind of you." He replaces the flat cap on his head. "Don't worry about it. I'm thkilled at falling on flat thurfaceth and up thtairs. Mighty thkilled, unfortunately."

"Pardon my lithp. My front theeth fell out. My mom thays they'll grow back. My thister Jean thays they won't becauth I fall thoo much you thee." Jackson shyly states.

"Anywhoo.. Enough gabbing on. Gramma thaid to thow you and your fwend around the farm, we have eggth to collect before dinner time or she will haf my hide!" declares Jackson.

Jackson leads them to the hen house after they cleaned up their lunch dishes. The hen house is as big as Alex's garage at home. It is right behind the farmhouse, on the other side of a beautiful flower garden. Jackson opens the door and shows them in.

"Now remember to clothe the doorth behind yah, or Jean will be mad. You don't wanna thee her mad!" He explains.

"Oh the smell!" The smell inside makes Alex gag. Jo smiles and pats her on the back.

11

"You will get used to it. Remember, our goal is buying those bikes for the summer."

Alex nods, finding Jo's reassurance comforting. Alex doesn't trust herself to open her mouth and speak. Alex isn't sure what will come out: words or her lunch?

Inside the hen house, they see rows and rows of shelves lining the wall, all the way to the ceiling. There is hay everywhere. There are little gangways connecting each level with chickens shuffling around everywhere. Two sets of ladders lean against the walls. They are sturdy looking, with wheels and a pedal on the bottom.

Jackson shows them how to lock down the breaks on the wheels of the ladders. Then he grabs a woven basket next to the front door and climbs up the ladder faster than a squirrel. He puts his hand into the nearest patch of hay and pulls out an egg. "Thee, eathy ath pie!" he exclaims. "Thith ith to not drop the eggth when you're done." He raises the basket towards them for emphasis.

"Mission egg hunting for summer bikes, go!" They each grab a basket, heading to the other ladder. Realizing only one can be on the ladder at a time they play rock paper scissors to see who will go up first.

Jo wins. Alex puts the break on and helps by holding the basket. Alex feels better now that she has a job to concentrate on rather than the awful smell.

It takes them all afternoon to collect all the eggs they can see. They move the ladder along the wall to reach all the different spots where they see eggs. It's a lot of fun trying to find them in the hay.

When Jo's arms hurt from looking for eggs, she swaps with Alex. They swapped many times. The last time they swapped places, Jo slips on the second to last stair on the way down, falling backwards on top of a very startled Alex. A big spray of hay goes everywhere. They disappear into the thick of it.

"Hey, you two alwight?" asks Jackson worriedly. Jumping down from the other ladder.

Jo replies "Yes, Jackson. I just missed a step…." then bursts into laughter when she sees all the hay stuck in Alex's curly hair.

"Oh, no." says Alex, "How bad is it?" she asked, putting her hands up and taking out some hay. Her eyes are as wide as a hungry hippo's mouth.

"You look hay-riffic," replies Jo, and they all burst into laughter.

"Scaring all the chickens, Jackson?" a voice from the front door startles them. They all turn, squinting. There is another girl there; she is pretty. She has beautiful thick and curly hair but then you see her face. Her face is scowling at them. Jo realizes it's Jean, Jackson's sister.

"Hello, Thith. You know Jo, thith is her fwend, Alex."

"Hello, troublemakers," Jean says, rolling her eyes. "Gramma says it's dinner time, have to lock up the hens." She is swinging a set of keys in her hand.

Alex recognizes Jean as one of Chantel's old classmates. The one Chantel refers to as Mean Jean. Startled by the revelation, Alex forgets the hay in her hair and grabs Jo by the arm and whispers "C'mon, let's go!" running out the door.

"What is the hurry, Alex? Are you alright?" asks Jo, when they finally reach the house.

"Yes, I'm fine. Don't you know who that is? That's Mean Jean! She is the real Mean Girl, from the movie. My sister doesn't like her. She pulled a mean prank on my sister. We best stay away." explains Alex.

"Don't worry, Alex. She is lonely, not mean, Mom says." Jo smiles and pats her on the back. "I met her last summer when I stayed with Gramma

Gladys. Jean and Jackson's parents make them work the farm in the summers. Something about building character."

Alex is not convinced. Chantel cried for days and did not want to go back to school. Mom had to bribe her to go back to school with chocolates and lots of hugs.

Jackson catches up to them at this point and mumbles an apology for his rude sister. They all file into the kitchen with their baskets full of eggs. Inside, they find Gramma Gladys cooking already. They proudly show her their collection of eggs.

"A wonderful job, my little bugs. I see Jackson showed you the ropes. Now these eggs are important." explains Gramma. "We will take them to the farmers market. I also have apples that need picking and selling, aren't you in luck? At the farmers market, I have arranged a table for you two next to mine. Since it will be your own business and my product we will make a deal. A business deal."

"Really?! That sounds like a great idea!" says Alex.

"Now hang on a minute. Dad says there is always a catch in a business deal," says Jo, trying very hard to act and sound like an adult.

"Good point, my little bug," responds Gramma Gladys with a wink. "Let's say 70% of what you sell will go to your bicycles and the rest will go to expenses. Expenses are paying the farmers market fees and packaging. I will show you how to package tomorrow. How does that sound?'

"What about 80% to the bicycles fund, and the rest to expenses?" asks Jo, again trying to sound as much like an adult as possible.

"You drive a good bargain, Miss Jo! What do you think Alex?" asks Gramma Gladys.

"I'm with Jo!" Alex responds, knocking the rest of the points out on her fingers. "We do all the picking, packaging and selling at the farmers market. You did the growing, you are also going to drive us, and you found us a table at the farmers market."

"Good thinking, Miss Jo and Miss Alex! You always have to look at the big picture," says Gramma Gladys triumphantly. "It's a deal." Gramma Gladys extends both of her hands, one to each girl.

"Yes! Thank you so much, Gramma!" says Jo, shaking her hand and sealing the deal.

"Thank you, Gramma Gladys. This is going to be so much fun!" chimes in Alex.

Jo and Alex give Gramma Gladys a hug. A plan to earn money for their bicycles is in motion.

The girls hope the farmers market will be busy. They promise each other that they would pick so many apples and eggs that their arms almost fall off, like the time they tried to wash cars.

Jo and Alex hear heavy boots coming down the hallway. Gramma Gladys is smiling. It's Grampa Mark; he has arrived for dinner!

"Heeeyy, look at you beauties!" says Grampa Mark, cap in hand with dirt-covered overalls. "I see you've spent some time in the hen house," he says while picking strands of hay from Alex's hair. "How about you girls go get a bath before dinner and we'll get to bed early. Tomorrow will be a full day."

"Oh Mark," says Gramma happily, walking over and planting a kiss on his cheek. "They were just telling me about the eggs they collected. They are going to sell them and some of the apples at the market with me. We made our business deal official; they plan on buying bicycles with the money they earn."

"Now there is an idea. Hard work for your toys. Good on yah. You'll appreciate them more," says Grampa Mark. "I'll race you two to the dinner table then. If I'm cleaned up first, you won't get any roasted potatoes!" He declares with a cheeky grin, disappearing down the hallway.

Jo and Alex got cleaned up for dinner as fast as they could. It takes them forever to get all the hay out of Alex's hair. Somehow, they still get to the dinner table first. Grampa Mark is nowhere to be found. Gramma Gladys is not smiling in the kitchen anymore. She chases them out of the kitchen when they offer to help. She tells them to set the table instead and then wait on the porch.

"Do you want to sit outside on the porch swing?" asks Jo when they are done setting the table. Alex agrees.

They settle in and slowly swing back and forth. Listening to the sounds of the farm is peaceful.

"I love your grandparents," says Alex.

"Yeah, they are pretty special. They met long ago when he was in the army and she was a nurse. He fell in love with Gramma and they came back to Gramma's family farm to start their own family. This is where my Mom grew up," explains Jo. "My Gramma helped me learn to read before school. She loves adventures too, almost as much as she loves --"

"Boooo!" yells Grampa Mark from behind their seat. The girls scream loudly, realizing too late that he snuck up behind them. Grampa Mark laughs a big bottom-of-the-belly type laugh. Jo smacks him on the shoulder.

"Oh Grampa Mark! My tummy hurts from laughing today, and now you scared us both!" teases Jo.

"Gotta keep your wits about ya, my little angel," responds Grampa Mark.

"Dinners ready, mac and cheese, green beans, and roast!" Gramma Gladys hollers down the hallway.

Jo turns to Grampa Mark and whispers, "What happened to the roasted potatoes?"

Bashful, a clean Grampa Mark looks at his feet, cap in hand.

"I may have scared your Gramma while you girls were getting cleaned up," responds Grampa Mark. "The potatoes flew everywhere. Gramma Gladys chased me out of the kitchen after that. So macaroni and cheese it is!"

All of them have a lovely meal with Gramma Gladys and Grampa Mark. Grampa Mark soon got Gramma Gladys to smile again with his stories. Grampa Mark loves telling stories.

Afterward, Jo and Alex take the dishes to the kitchen and wash them. Gramma Gladys said at dinner that every time they do the dishes they will earn another $5 towards their bicycle fund. While the girls are busy in the kitchen, Jo hears Gramma Gladys ask about Bessie.

"Bessie is a strong one, my love. She'll be fine," says Grampa Mark. "Time for a cup of hot tea?"

"Yes, thank you dear." responds Gramma Gladys. "We should see if Jo and Alex want to learn how to look after the little calf?"

"Good idea," says Grampa Mark gently. "I'll show them how tomorrow."

Jo is very excited. Her Mom told her stories of looking after calves and lambs on the farm and how cute they are, but that you should always be careful with your fingers because they nip them really fast. She thinks Alex will enjoy it a lot. Alex is always so kind to everyone, including animals.

CHAPTER TWO

Jo is a morning person. Alex is *not* a morning person.

In the mornings, Alex's curly hair always looks like she stuck her finger in an electrical outlet. Her older sister, Chantel, calls her the little monster because all her responses sound like growls when she first wakes up. Chantel teases her that it will get easier when Alex is a teenager. Alex doubts it. Alex misses Chantel.

Jo, on the other hand, wakes up looking happy. She always has a grin on her face and a spring in her step, even before breakfast! Alex wishes she could be more like Jo.

Alex woke up on her first morning on the farm very abruptly. A chicken landed right on her tummy while she was sleeping. By the time she realized it was there, she opened her eyes to a "pok pok pok" sound and a tickly feeling as it stepped across her tummy. The chicken was staring at her! Alex lay very still.

Alex's first thought is, *How dangerous are chickens? Will it poke my eyes out?*

"Umph… I see you've made a new friend," says Jo, bouncing onto the bed. The chicken is startled, jumps off the bed, and starts poking at the ground with her beak. Alex nods. Jo thinks it is funny. Alex does not.

"How did she get in?" asks Alex while eyeing the chicken.

"A fox got in the hen house last night. Scattered them all over the farm," explains Jo, matter of factly. "Foxes eat hens. Jackson and Mr. Sam have been collecting them since early this morning. Time to join the fun, Alex! Get up!"

Alex thinks the chicken would be a cute pet. Especially since she woke her up nicer than Chantel ever did. Chickens are definitely better than cats and dogs.

Today is their first full day on the farm. Jo and Alex found identical jean overalls by their suitcases. They rushed downstairs for breakfast and then outside to meet Grampa Mark for the morning chores.

On the way out the front door, Jo and Alex find two pairs of mud boots by the front door. One is red and one is blue. Jo and Alex are so excited. Together their adventures are always fun!

Mr. Sam pulls up and tells them to hop on the truck. Jo, Alex, and Jackson hop onto the back. They all head for the old barn on the other side of the grazing fields.

Mr. Sam is kind and very good with animals. He has worked on the farm longer than Jo has been alive. Mom says Mr. Sam is family; the family you choose. He doesn't have the same name or Gramma as them, but they all work and live together. Mr. Sam always says he prefers animals over people; animals are always kind. Jule is his favorite animal. She helps herd the sheep and keep the foxes away when they are out of the pen. If Jule isn't with the sheep she's usually following Mr. Sam around.

"Where is Grampa Mark?" asks Alex.

"I guess he had one too many nightcaps," explains Mr. Sam.

Mr. Sam laughs at their confused expressions and slaps his leg with his hand. "It's time to check on Old Bessie, then show you how to pick those apples. Let's go!"

The chicken from earlier appears out of nowhere. She follows Alex around like Jule follows Mr. Sam. Alex decides to name her Rosie. She likes the chicken, even if she chooses to wake her up really early every morning.

Bessie was doing well when they checked on her. Mr. Sam said Gramma Gladys would be keeping an eye on the newborn calf to make sure it gets enough food. Jo and Alex are surprised at how BIG Bessie is. They were only as tall as her mouth, which was just the right height to rub her nose gently through the fence.

Mr. Sam drove them to the apple orchard afterward. He gave them wide straw hats, a small wheelbarrow each that had tiny holes in it, and two big bottles of water. He also explained that when they heard the bell ring from the farmhouse, it would be time to come up and grab some food. Jackson, Jo, and Alex are excited.

After a morning spent with their arms above their heads, they heard the bell. Jo, Alex, and Jackson trotted their way back to the farmhouse for lunch. Sunburnt red with sticky hands, they wondered how many apples it would take to buy a bike.

"My arms are going to fall off. How will I steer a bicycle, Alex?" asks a gloomy faced Jo.

"Cheer up," interrupts Jackson. "You girlth did great today! Tell you what. If the weather ith nithe, we could roatht marthmellowth tonight."

"Thank you, Jackson," responds Alex. "That sounds great! I love marshmallows… but would Gramma Gladys let us build a fire and roast them?"

Jackson responds with excitement in his voice, "We won't know if we don't ask, right?"

The idea of roasting marshmallows cheers Jo up. Jo likes marshmallows. Especially when you get to roast them until they turn black.

Gramma Gladys is waiting for the girls on the porch. She is reading a book when they arrive for lunch.

"I see you found your farm clothes, my little bugs," says Gramma Gladys. She closes the book and stands up. "Every lady has to have nice shoes. Now round the back you go! You won't be trekking sticky apple droppings through the house."

Jo, Alex, and Jackson are hungry. They all run around the back. Alex trips over Rosie the chicken again on her way.

Jackson stops to help her up. Jackson had a toothless grin on his face.

"Good 'ta know I ain't the only one who ith thkilled at falling on flat thurfaceth," says Jackson.

After lunch, Gramma Gladys gives them strict instructions to put on their hats before leaving the house. Otherwise, they will look like lobsters at sunset!

They all do as Gramma Gladys says, putting their hats on with a smile.

Jackson decides to show them the other animals on the farm; he organizes a bag of treats from Gramma and guides them to the pond. He declares proudly that they are going to go a roundabout way back to the orchard.

First, they find ducks. The ducks are spread out near the pond. Some ducks are paddling quietly across its surface. Other ducks are sleeping on the grass. They are the cutest little duckies ever!

Alex and Jo notice a mother duck with her ducklings. The ducks swim to shore and dry themselves on the bank. The mother duck spreads her wings and shakes her feathers, wiggling her whole body. Alex and Jo think that's funny. They try doing it too. Jackson giggles.

Jackson pulls out slices of bread, gives some to Alex and Jo, then breaks tiny pieces of his own. He holds the bread in the palm of his hand and slowly approaches the mother duck.

Alex and Jo eagerly watch the mother duck as she notices Jackson for the first time. She ruffles her feathers in warning before noticing the bread in Jackson's hand. Jackson stops and squats while stretching his hand slowly towards the mother duck.

The mother duck checks on her ducklings, then slowly approaches. She pecks the bread right out of his hand! The ducklings see that their mom trusts Jackson, so they crowd around him too.

Jackson motions for Jo and Alex to join. The girls slowly sit on either side of him. They giggle at the peck feeling the ducklings make when picking up the bread. The ducklings sometimes miss and then it feels like a slight pinch. It doesn't hurt though. It's actually funny to Jo and Alex.

Alex decides that ducks are her next favorite animal, right up there with friendly chickens like Rosie. Alex finished feeding the bread she had to the ducks first. She looks up and notices a few geese paddling over the pond towards them. They are bigger, with longer necks and strange black eyes. One of them opens its large beak and squawks. It sounds similar to the sound Alex heard in the car on the drive in. Alex bumps Jackson on the shoulder and points to the geese.

"Are they friendly?" asks Alex innocently.

"No ma'am!" Jackson responds hurriedly. He throws the bag of goodies over his shoulder, smacking Jo on the head and yells, "Ith time to go!"

Jackson is running down the road quickly, racing past an old tractor which looks like it would make a great jungle gym. Jo and Alex run after him. They run until they can't breathe anymore, and then run some more. Jackson ran and held onto his flat cap the entire way to the horse barn. All the girls could see ahead of them was a bouncing head of black hair and dust from the road. Jo and Alex tried their best to keep up.

Jackson is really fast. When they finally caught up to him, they put their hands on their knees and try to catch their breath. Jackson's face is bright red, Alex's legs feel like jelly, and then Jo starts laughing!

Alex looks at her like she is crazy. *How does she have the air to laugh!?*

"I forgot you didn't like the geese, Jackson," says Jo, in between breathless giggles.

CHAPTER THREE

The rest of the animals of the farm were kind. The horses were slow and charming. They ate bits of carrots right out of the girl's hands. Jo thought it would be funny and started walking like the geese everywhere they went. Jackson did not like the joke as much as the girls did, so they stopped.

Grampa Mark drove past them in the big tractor once on the route around the farm. He was pale and wore dark sunglasses.

He shouted, "Lookie here, it's the four troublemakers!"

They did not understand what he meant by four of them until they turned around to look behind them. Rosie the chicken was not far behind Alex. Alex really liked the chicken. Rosie seemed to like Alex too.

On the way past the barn, the girls were talking to Jackson about his favorite books.

"I like bookth about thpace." says Jackson. "My favowite would be anything at all about the galaxy. I'm gonna be an exthplorer one day!"

Neither Jo nor Alex have ever read books about space. They both want to see what the excitement is all about. Maybe they'll want to become space explorers too!

Jackson is nice. If Jackson likes those types of books, then they should too.

Jackson, Jo, and Alex keep walking to the orchard. They pass the pen with all the pigs and wonder where Mr. Sam is.

"What is that smell – EWWWW!" Jo disappears from where she was walking next to Alex and Jackson.

Jo did not look where she was going and walked straight into a pile of horse poop.

"Ewwww!" shouts Jo again, from the ground. She fell because her boot got stuck in it!

Alex and Jackson are surprised. Jackson grabs her arms and Alex pulls on Jo's boot. Jo is not a happy camper, but Jackson and Alex think it is funny.

Jackson found a watering hose and cleaned off Jo's boot so that they could continue on to the orchard.

Finally, they all arrive back at the orchard. The apples from this morning were still safely in their wheelbarrows and they continued to pick more. The day dragged on but soon they heard the dinner bell.

When they returned to the farmhouse with their wheelbarrows full of apples, Gramma Gladys was so proud. She couldn't believe how many they had picked in one day.

Jackson asked, "Thince we did thoe well, can we roath marthmallowth tonight Gramma?"

"That's a lovely idea, Jackson," said Gramma Gladys, clapping her hands together with glee. "How about you all go wash up so we can have some dinner, and then we will start the marshmallow roast?"

Jackson, Jo, and Alex were so happy! This was the best day ever. They worked hard, saw lots of cute animals, were chased by geese, fed some ducks, stepped in a pile of poop and now they were going to roast marshmallows. Now Alex understood why Jo enjoyed coming here so much!

For dinner Jackson, Mr. Sam, and Jean joined them. It was a lovely meal, but Jo and Alex are worried about all the extra dishes. Jean surprises them by being very kind. She joins them in the kitchen and helps to dry the dishes. Jo and Alex are thankful she decided to help. They invite Jean to join them at the marshmallow roast.

While Jo, Alex, and Jean were doing the dishes from dinner, Jackson and Grampa Mark gathered firewood from the back of the house. When they were done with the dishes, Jo and Alex grabbed the marshmallows and joined everyone for a beautiful bonfire under the starry night sky. Gramma Gladys brought blankets for everyone to sit on.

Grampa Mark and Mr. Sam go to the porch. They sit there all evening talking and sharing stories from their childhood.

The bonfire is beautiful. Alex has never seen so many stars at night in her life. The stars stretch from horizon to horizon. The sky looks like someone had taken a saltshaker and thrown it in the air, with all the salt bits sticking in the sky. The sky is stunning!

Jo loves nights like this on the farm. The fire is warm, the marshmallows are yummy, and friends nearby. She is happy to share this with Alex.

Once Jo, Alex, and Jackson finish their marshmallows. Gramma Gladys shows them how to lie down and watch the stars on their blankets. Gramma Gladys explains that after a few minutes they would be able to see something spectacular.

They waited… and waited... and waited. Nothing was happening. Then Alex saw it!

"Oh look! I see it. Like a bright light that ran across the sky then disappeared!? Is that it, Gramma Gladys?" asked Alex excitedly, sitting up and looking over at Gramma Gladys eagerly.

"Yes my dear," Gramma Gladys smiled back encouragingly. "That is a shooting star. Now close your eyes and make a wish, my little bug."

Alex did exactly that.

I wish for bicycles for Jo and I. One red and one blue, with ribbons on the handles!

Alex opened her eyes and found Rosie there, again! Alex laughed and patted Rosie the chicken lightly on her back.

"Well, what did you wish for?" whispered Jo.

"Now now, girls. You know better than that Jo," interrupted Gramma Gladys. "If she tells you her wish it won't come true!"

"Sorry, Gramma," says Jo disappointedly, lying back down to stare at the stars.

Alex grabs Jo's hand and gives it a reassuring squeeze.

Alex whispers just quietly enough for only Jo's ears, "Don't worry, you'll like it when it comes true!" then lies back down next to Jo.

Jo finds that comforting. Alex really is the bestest best friend in the whole world!

They lie there watching the stars until their eyes start dropping, for they are so sleepy from their adventures today. Gramma Gladys hurries them off to bed while Grampa Mark puts out the fire.

The days fly by with sunny skies, animal noises, sticky apples, and eggs covered in hay. Wherever they went, Rosie was not far behind. Jackson greeted them at the back door every day after breakfast and stayed for dinner most nights. After dinner, they would package the goods they collected that day.

Today they were at the farmers market. The farmers market was so busy!

Why are there so many smells on farms and at farmers markets? thinks Alex.

Gramma Gladys sends Alex and Jo to explore before it gets busy. People roam from table to table, shouting hellos across their tables and greeting old friends with warm hugs. Cooked meals of eggs and bacon waft over to them from the other stalls as they eagerly walk along the well trampled path. Another table displays cinnamon pancakes, freshly baked breads, and more pastries than either of the girls had ever seen.

Further on the path, there is a lady with flowers in her hair, fanny pack on her hip and a spring in her step. She sees the girls and offers them a sunflower each.

Jo and Alex beam with smiles of delight. They accept with thanks and run back to show Gramma Gladys their treasures. Jo and Alex decide to display the beautiful sunflowers on their table. One on each end.

"It is a little sunshine to give everyone happiness when they come to our table!" declares Jo happily.

In their ponytails and floppy hats, they smile at everyone who walks past.

The girls made signs with prices for their apples and eggs that are displayed on the table. Jo and Alex, with Jackson's help of course, had collected so much that Grampa Mark and Mr. Sam had to help them load the truck early this morning. The truck was almost full! The table was right next to Gramma Gladys' table at the farmers market.

Jo and Alex were ready to sell their goods. Together, Jo and Alex greeted people as they walked by with a smile and great big hello's. In the beginning, they only sold a few apples and one tray of eggs. Jo and Alex were beginning to think their dreams of buying bicycles would be over. No summer rides for them.

Gramma Gladys came up with an idea. She gave them copies of the recipes for the goods she sold at her table. She told the girls to offer them to people, or that they could have it with their purchase. She called it a cross-promotion; a bonus for the customers.

Alex admired the way Gramma Gladys spoke to everyone that came to visit her table. She remembered little details about their families, how they were doing, and what they liked to buy. Jo said it was because Gramma Gladys cares. Jo and Alex copied the way Gramma Gladys was kind to people. They didn't know much about the strange new people, but they did try their best to be kind.

Jo and Alex soon sold all their inventory. They were so excited! After counting the money they made for the day they realized they were halfway to their goal! Gramma Gladys told them that part of their expense was to pay the market for their spot there. It works out that 10% of their expenses would go to the market, and the other 10% would go to her for fuel and growing the goods.

Gramma Gladys said they could go play with some of the other children their age who were playing on the playground not far from where they were selling their goods. Jo and Alex watched from afar before approaching. The kids were spinning around until they were dizzy and then raced towards a huge tree nearby. Once they reached the tree everyone would giggle, turn around, and run back. The first one back to home base got to sit in the cool shade near home base and command the beginning of the next race.

On the third time before they restarted the game, Alex and Jo gripped hands and walked forward to say hello.

"Can we play?" asked Jo bravely.

"Yes, of course. But it's a race!" said a freckle-faced girl happily. "My name is Tara."

"I am Jo and this Alex," responded Jo.

Jo and Alex lost track of time playing with their new friends. Eventually, they realized more and more children started playing with them. There were also more and more people around. Jo and Alex say goodbye to their new friends and head back to their table next to Gramma Gladys.

Gramma Gladys showed them where to pay the man of the market and then directed them to help pack what was left of her goods onto the truck.

Gramma Gladys drives them back to the farm. She toots the horn of the truck multiple times before getting out. Jo and Alex cover their ears, watching as Rosie the chicken squawks off the porch and waddles away.

"Coming dear!" shouts Grampa Mark as he walks out the farmhouse towards them. He makes a funny face at Gramma Gladys. They laugh, then he helps them unpack what's left of their farmers market adventure.

CHAPTER FOUR

The next few days were a blur. They flew by so fast! Alex and Jo spent most of their time with Jackson working on the farm. They enjoy being outside and seeing the animals every day.

Jo's favorite thing to do is feeding the ducks.

Alex likes it when Rosie follows her around.

Jackson enjoys having friends to play with.

Every day after breakfast they start by collecting the eggs and checking on Bessie. After that, they feed the horses, say hello to ducks without the geese catching them, and then continue on to the apple orchard. By dinner time they are usually exhausted as they pack their eggs and apples for the next farmers market.

Most days, Grampa Mark would make every effort to sneak up on them and give them a fright. Jo, Alex, and Jackson got better at catching Grampa Mark in the act as he tried sneaking up to scare them.

One humid afternoon the sun was so hot they were dripping with sweat. As the day went on, it got hotter and hotter. By the end of the day, Jo,

Alex, and Jackson were sticky from picking apples again.

Jo reached up for one of the last ripe looking apples and missed; it fell off the tree and onto her face instead. Bruised and sore Jo was mad and embarrassed. Jo picked up the ripe apple and threw it at Jackson. Jackson ducked, laughing. Jackson thought it was funny. Then Jackson picked up a rather squishy looking apple and threw it at Alex. That is how the happiest apple war in the world started.

Jo, Alex, and Jackson started running around, dodging in between trees and picking the ripest apples off the ground. Some were so squishy and old that they fell into pieces when thrown.

Alex had really good aim.

Jo was really slow, but she somehow was always laughing.

Jackson threw one rotten apple at Jo, but Jo ducked and it landed on Alex instead! Splattering down Alex's shirt and dropping triumphantly to the ground. The girls surrendered after that. Jackson won! Jackson is so happy.

Dinner was lovely that evening. They had Alex's favorite: roasted chicken and vegetables served on rice with a creamy cheese sauce.

"Thank you for a lovely dinner, Gramma Gladys," says Alex.

"You are very welcome, my dear," responds Gramma Gladys. "Grampa Mark prepared the roasted chicken tonight. He is really handy with chicken."

Jo stops mid-bite, looking down at the plate. Jo looks up at Grandpa Mark and then toward Alex. Jo shakes her head and then continues enjoying the meal. Grampa Mark sees Jo's reaction and then scratches his head as if realizing something. Gramma Gladys saw sorrow in his eyes. Gramma Gladys looks confused.

"I have a little surprise for you two girls." says Grampa Mark when they finished dinner dishes that night. "Follow me!"

Grampa Mark takes them down the hallway and opens the door to the sunroom. In it the girls see books. Books of every shape, size, and age. They lined the walls from the roof to the floor.

"I hear you girls have a love of books." said Grampa Mark. "Well, you are welcome to pick one at a time and read them during your stay here."

"Thank you, Grampa Mark!" chime the girls in unison. Jo and Alex both give Grampa Mark a hug to say thank you.

Jo and Alex spend the rest of the evening looking through and choosing books to read. Soon they find a seat on the porch swing together. Jo and Alex get drawn into their own worlds of black and white text until Gramma Gladys brings them a cup of hot tea and sends them to bed.

Alex was not woken up by Rosie this morning.
Instead, Jo is sitting at the end of her bed looking concerned. Jo is wringing her hands. Alex props herself up on her arms.

"Are you alright Jo?" asks Alex, drowsily wiping her eyes.

"Yes, are you?" responds Jo with concern. She is biting her nails.

"Yes, a bit sleepy still. Why are you biting your nails?" asks Alex.

"I am not!" says Jo and sits on her hands defiantly. "I was just trying to wake you up, lazybones! Now get out of bed, we have work to do.

Tomorrow is our last market day." She hops off the bed and runs to the bathroom to get changed.

Alex is left confused and wonders, *What has gotten into Jo?*

Jo looked like she was in a bad mood. Jo was behaving like Chantel does when Mom says she couldn't do something. Alex gets dressed and heads downstairs to breakfast with Jo.

Jean is at breakfast today. There is no sign of Jackson. Gramma Gladys says she needs help with Bessie's calf. Gramma Gladys asks for all the girls to help. Jean starts to protest but Gramma Gladys stops her by holding up her hand.

"You hear me, young lady," warns Gramma Gladys angrily, "We all eat well off this farm, you have to give back and care for those in need too. You will learn how to, but if you never choose to use those skills then so be it. Either way, you will respect the rules, understand Miss Jean?"

"Yes ma'am," responds a deflated Jean.

Jo and Alex clean up breakfast dishes while Gramma Gladys and Jean get the supplies ready to feed the calf. Together they head over to the barn. Gramma Gladys asks Jean to clean out the water trough and for Jo to sweep the old hay out.

"Grab that bottle, my little bug," Gramma Gladys tells Alex.

Alex is so happy to be called a little bug too that she rushes to pick up the bottle and hand it to Gramma Gladys, startling the young calf in the process.

"Shhh," says Gramma Gladys to the calf to calm her down, patting her softly.

"I'm sorry!" whispers Alex, realizing she startled the young calf.

"It's okay, just make slow movements," explains Gramma Gladys. "Now come here, sit on this stool next to me and I will show you how to feed her some milk."

Alex happily obliges. Gramma Gladys shows her how to hold up the bottle so the calf can suck out the milk, as she instructs to hold it higher than its head. Alex does exactly as she is told. The calf is so cute and clumsy! Next, Jo tries it and then so does Jean when she finishes filling the water trough.

When they are done feeding the calf, Jo and Alex go to the orchard. They pick as many apples as they can fit in their wheelbarrows. Jackson did not join them today. They don't know where Jackson is.

After the orchard, they head to the hen house and collect all the eggs. This time Jo and Alex each have a ladder to work on. Mean Jean arrives when the dinner bell rings and tells them to leave and to stop wasting her time.

"Why are you so mean?" says Alex boldly. "You can see we are trying to collect eggs to sell here. It's for our bicycle fund."

"Mean!? I am not mean," says Jean. "Stop wasting my time and get out of here. Now!"

"No, you were mean to my sister, Chantel. She cried for days!" shouts Alex. "What did you say to her?"

Jean smirks confidently, "Nothing that wasn't true, little girl. Mind your own business."

Jo notices that Alex is so mad that her fists are balled. Jo does the first thing that comes to mind. Jo walks up to Jean slowly and smiles. Jo then puts her arms around Jean and hugs her.

Alex is uncomfortable and shocked.

Alex thinks, *Why is Jo hugging Mean Jean, someone who hurt her sister's feelings?*

Jo leans back and looks up at Jean. "Sometimes we all just need a hug to feel better again. Time to go Alex." They then walk out the door with their baskets of eggs.

Jo and Alex spend the rest of the day packing their eggs and apples. The girls are excited to go to the farmers market. Maybe they will see Tara again? They hope so. After dinner, Jean finds them on the porch reading.

"I have something to say," says Jean.

Jo and Alex put down their books and pay full attention to Jean.

"I am sorry for hurting your sisters' feelings, Alex. I will call and tell her myself later,'' says Jean. "I am jealous of how well Jo and you get along. I don't make friends very easily. Can we all be friends please?"

"Yes! We would love to be your friend," responds Jo, as she elbows Alex in the ribs.

"Fine," says Alex. Crossing her arms indignantly.

"Would you like to read to us?" asks Jo.

"No thank you. It is bedtime. See you in the morning," says Jean.

The next morning they go to the farmers market with Gramma Gladys again. This time they have double the stock of what they had last time. Jo, Alex, and Jackson had a lot more time to collect apples and eggs. Jo and Alex are very proud of their accomplishment!

Alex has an idea.

"Gramma Gladys, what if we walked around the farmers market and introduced ourselves to the customers? We could be nice and let them know what we sell. That way if they are looking for the items we have, they know then where to buy it," asks Alex.

"Well, that is a great idea!" Gramma Gladys responds. "Off you go! I will look after your table until you get back. You can play with the other kids if you'd like as well." Gramma winks to them as they turn and run away.

Jo and Alex see people of all shapes and sizes as they go. At every table they stop to say hi to customers, and they take turns with who talks first because they are shy. Together, they overcome their shyness and support each other. When they get to the end of the walkway, they find themselves in the children's play area.

Jo and Alex find Tara and continue with their fun games from last week. This farmers market is really fun! Jo and Alex wish they could have shared it with Jackson. Jackson likes adventures too. They try not to get their boots dirty.

On the way back they check that each other's ponytails still look pretty. Satisfied, Jo and Alex go back to selling their goods at the farmers market.

Jo and Alex sold out again; everything went! All the eggs and all the apples are gone. It was like people remembered they were there from last week. Jo and Alex were so happy to see familiar faces buy from them.

By the end of the farmers market, their money box was full and their smiles were big. They went by themselves and paid the man of the farmers market 10% of what they earned and another 10% went to Gramma Gladys. Jo and Alex had sold over 80 trays of eggs and 10 wheelbarrows of apples, by their estimates. Gramma Gladys was beaming with pride as they rode home that day.

They helped Gramma Gladys and Grampa Mark unload the truck when they got back to the farm. When they finish, Jo and Alex go in search of Jackson to tell him the good news.

CHAPTER FIVE

Jackson was nowhere to be found. Jo and Alex are worried about him. They looked for him by the ducks, in the barn where Bessie was, in the hen house, and around the orchard. Jackson was not in any of those places! Jo and Alex went back to the farmhouse to look for Gramma. They found her in the sunroom with the books.

"Gramma, we can't find Jackson. He isn't with the ducks, or Bessie, or in the hen house, or even in the orchard!" Jo said while waving her hands in a temper of worry.

Gramma peered over the top of her red-rimmed glasses. The silence in the room stretched awkwardly.

"Watch your manners, and please rephrase your question, my little bug," says Gramma Gladys promptly.

"Please Gramma Gladys, do you know where Jackson is?" says a worried Jo. "We are very worried about him. We can't find him anywhere! "

"Last I saw Jackson he was by the old tractor at the pond," responds Gramma Gladys. She then returns to reading her book.

Jo and Alex are confused. They hurry off in the direction of the old tractor.

"Why do you think Jackson didn't come to say hi when we arrived, Jo?" asks a concerned Alex.

"I don't know, it is very unlike him," responds Jo.

Jo and Alex found Jackson sitting quietly by the old tractor. There is a small saucer of milk in front of him, he is staring at it closely. Jo and Alex are very confused. Alex notices that Jackson is sitting the same way he does when he feeds the ducklings. Before Alex can tell Jo, Jo tries to talk to Jackson.

"Jackson, what are you doing? Are you okay?" asks Jo.

"Hello ladieth," Jackson shyly responds. This time he does not take his hat off in his usual greeting. Alex notices that his hair is not as puffy as hers anymore.

"Did you get a haircut, Jackson?" blurts out Alex. Jackson twitches; by his reaction it is clear he does not like the subject.

"Yeah, my Mom thaid I had too," explains Jackson. "The lady pulled my hair, it hurt. But Ma sayth we have to, becauthe a man should alwayth look neat. Then I tried tah remind her that I'm still jutht a boy. My mom jutht thmiled and kithed me

50

on the head. Then the hair lady kept on cutting my hair."

Jackson is clearly embarrassed. He points to the old tractor. "I found a kitty, I am thcared of the foxeth getting it."

Alex and Jo decide to ignore the haircut and help with trying to get the kitten out from underneath the old tractor. They sit and wait patiently. The quiet seems to help Jackson. Instead of sitting with his arms crossed, he slowly relaxes. The kitty makes an appearance after what feels like most of the afternoon.

The kitten peeks its black and white head out from underneath the old tractor. It has pretty blue eyes and its whiskers move back and forth. The kitten meows and then slowly crawls towards the saucer of milk.

Jackson smiles. The kitten stops licking up the milk and looks up at Jackson. Jackson looks relieved. Jo and Alex look at each other; neither is sure what to do. Jackson pats the kitten and then slowly picks it up.

Jo, Alex, and Jackson take it back to the farmhouse where Gramma Gladys makes a little bed for it. The kitten curls up and goes to sleep. Gramma Gladys shoes them out of the farmhouse, saying the kitten needs peace and quiet.

Jo and Alex finally tell Jackson their good news. Jackson is so happy for them he forgets about his haircut ordeal.

"Has anybody seen Rosie?" asks Alex. Jackson and Jo look at the floor, clearly uncomfortable.

Thankfully at this point, Jean arrives and asks to play with them. Jackson looks uneasily at the girls, worried they might fight.

Alex lifts her chin confidently in the air and declares, "Yes, we would love to play with you!"

Jo smiles at her best friend in the whole wide world, Alex. Jo is proud that Alex has decided to be nice. Jo shocks Alex when she gives her a big hug, then grabs Jean and Alex's hand and rushes to the orchard to play.

Jackson tells Jo to get in one wheelbarrow and Alex to get into another with Jean pushing. They raced through orchards, all the way to the other side. The speed humps from the rotten apples were squishy and made pushing the wheelbarrow very exciting. It weaved back and forth as the person in the wheelbarrow navigated through the little speed humps.

The wheelbarrows fell over a lot. They laughed, then got back in and tried again. Soon they were sticky from head to toe, more so than any day of apple picking in the orchard ever made them. Jo and Jackson win!

Alex and Jean squish rotten apples in their hair for the crowning.

Before long, they heard the dinner bell. Rushing back to the farmhouse, the four children laugh all the way there. They have a lovely family dinner and discuss all the places they can go to buy bicycles with their bicycle fund.

Jo's Mom and Dad arrived to pick up the girls today. They packed up their bags and cleaned their mud boots by the door. Jo and Alex were sad to leave the farm. They enjoyed looking after all the animals and going to the market.

Jo and Alex trudged out the front door to find Gramma Gladys and Grampa Mark. They are waiting on the front porch.

"Here you go my two little bugs," Gramma Gladys says as she offers them an envelope each with money. "This is all the money you made. Congratulations!

Jo and Alex give them both a hug and say thanks for having them and for helping them save for their bicycles. Jo and Alex have never seen so much money!

Jo's Mom is waiting in the car for them. Jo and Alex look around for Jackson and Jean. They are nowhere to be seen.
Jo and Alex load their suitcases in the back of the car. When they close the trunk, they hear the sound of people running. Turning around they see Jackson and Jean running down the road. Jean is wearing a pretty dress and Jackson a white shirt and dress pants.

Jo realizes they have their Sunday clothes on. Jackson waves at them excitedly as they run towards them. Jackson proceeds to fall on his face, ruining his Sunday best clothes right before they are supposed to go to church.

Jackson blushes as his sister Jean helps him up and dusts off his clothes.

Jo and Alex rush over to meet them.

Jackson blushes. The girls laugh and Jean smiles at all three of them fondly.

"Don't worry Jackson," Jean says encouragingly, "We will make a stop by the house to get another shirt for you."

Jackson looks up at his sister Jean with an appreciative smile on his face. He looks happy.

"We wanted to thay goodbye before you leave!" says a shy Jackson.

"Thank you! We are going to miss you both," says Jo. "It was really sweet to help us pick apples and collect the eggs we needed to sell. Hopefully we can see you again soon?"

"Yeah, we will be coming to the coatht this thummer, my mom told me today," says Jackson confidently.

"This is for you Jackson," says Jo as she hands him some of the cash from her envelope. "Thank you for your help with our bicycle fund. Maybe you can buy yourself a new flat cap?"

"That is a wonderful idea!" says Alex. "Be sure to bring your bicycles when you visit so we can all ride together!"

They nod, give each other hugs, and say their last goodbyes. When the car drives down the old dirt road, Jo and Alex look out the back window and wave goodbye to their friends. Jo is very happy Alex got to meet Jackson and Jean. She is very excited about what their summer adventures are going to be like on their new bicycles.

Alex can see why Jo enjoys the farm so much. Alex still wonders where Rosie went. She couldn't find her anywhere. Alex really hopes a Fox did not get Rosie. Anyway, Alex is excited for her wish to come true. Tomorrow they can buy their bicycles!

"Mom! I learned patience at Gramma Gladys'!" says Jo over breakfast the next morning. "Oh really?!" says her Mom. "What happened?" "Well, we picked so many apples my arms nearly fell off. Alex and Jackson became friends. Jackson taught us how to wait for ducklings to come close to feed them, and it works with kittens too! Alex was also kind to Mean Jean. Oops! I meant just Jean," responds Jo.

"That is wonderful news, sweetie," replies Mom.

Alex comes running through the front door of Jo's house.

"Hello ma'am," says Alex. "Is it time to go yet?"

Jo's Mom laughs and grabs her handbag and her car keys. "Yes it is, sweetie."

Jo and Alex jump and shout with delight. Jo's Mom drives them to the closest bicycle shop. Jo and Alex are overwhelmed by their choices! Jo and Alex saved so much money that they have a lot of options. They earned all this money by selling apples, eggs, and by doing the dishes at Gramma Gladys'.

Jo and Alex count their money again and again. Between the two of them, they can also afford matching helmets and knee pads too!

Alex chooses a blue bicycle with matching helmet and knee pads.

Jo chooses a red bicycle with matching helmet and knee pads.

They both also get matching white ribbons at the end of their handlebars! The girls are so excited about the great adventures they are going to have on their new bicycles.

Alex is beaming.

"Guess what Jo?" says Alex.

"What, Alex?" responds Jo.

"My wish on the shooting star came true!" says Alex.

Where should they go first?
To the beach? Or maybe to the park? Maybe they
should just race along the boardwalk!
This is going to be the best summer of their lives,
wherever their bicycles take them.

Made in the USA
Middletown, DE
10 September 2020